THE ART OF THE NOVELLA

THE
DISTRACTED
PREACHER

THE DISTRACTED PREACHER

THOMAS HARDY

MELVILLE HOUSE
BROOKLYN · LONDON

THE DISTRACTED PREACHER BY THOMAS HARDY

FIRST APPEARED IN *HARPER'S WEEKLY*, NEW YORK,
AND *NEW QUARTERLY MAGAZINE*, LONDON, 1879

© 2012 MELVILLE HOUSE PUBLISHING

FIRST MELVILLE HOUSE PRINTING: JUNE 2012

MELVILLE HOUSE PUBLISHING
145 PLYMOUTH STREET
BROOKLYN, NY 11201

WWW.MHPBOOKS.COM

ISBN: 978-1-61219-111-9

BOOK DESIGN: CHRISTOPHER KING, BASED ON
A SERIES DESIGN BY DAVID KONOPKA

PRINTED IN THE UNITED STATES OF AMERICA

1 2 3 4 5 6 7 8 9 10

LIBRARY OF CONGRESS CATALOGING-IN-PUBLICATION DATA:
A CATALOG RECORD IS AVAILABLE FROM THE LIBRARY OF CONGRESS

THE DISTRACTED PREACHER

CHAPTER I
HOW HIS COLD WAS CURED

Something delayed the arrival of the Wesleyan minister, and a young man came temporarily in his stead. It was on the thirteenth of January, 183-, that Mr. Stockdale, the young man in question, made his humble entry into the village, unknown, and almost unseen. But when those of the inhabitants who styled themselves of his connection became acquainted with him, they were rather pleased with the substitute than otherwise, though he had scarcely as yet acquired ballast of character sufficient to steady the consciences of the hundred and forty Methodists of pure blood who, at this time, lived in Nether-Moynton, and to give in addition supplementary support to the mixed race which went to church in the morning and chapel in the evening, or when there was a tea—as many as a hundred and ten people more, all told, and including the parish-clerk in the winter-time, when it was too dark for the vicar to observe who passed up the street at seven o'clock—which, to be just to him, he was never anxious to do.

It was owing to this overlapping of creeds that the celebrated population-puzzle arose among the denser gentry of the district around Nether-Moynton; how could it be that a parish containing fifteen score of strong full-grown Episcopalians, and nearly thirteen score of well-matured Dissenters, numbered barely two-and-twenty score adults in all?

The young man being personally interesting, those with whom he came in contact were content to waive for a while the graver question of his sufficiency. It is said that at this time of his life his eyes were affectionate, though without a ray of levity; that his hair was curly, and his figure tall; that he was, in short, a very lovable youth, who won upon his female hearers as soon as they saw and heard him, and caused them to say, "Why didn't we know of this before he came, that we might have gied him a warmer welcome!"

The fact was that, knowing him to be only provisionally selected, and expecting nothing remarkable in his person or doctrine, they and the rest of his flock in Nether-Moynton had felt almost as indifferent about his advent as if they had been the soundest church-going parishioners in the country, and he their true and appointed parson. Thus when Stockdale set foot in the place nobody had secured a lodging for him, and though his journey had given him a bad cold in the head, he was forced to attend to that business himself. On inquiry he found that the only possible accommodation in the village would be found at the house of one Mrs. Lizzy Newberry, at the upper end of the street.

It was a youth who gave this information, and Stockdale asked him who Mrs. Newberry might be.

The boy said that she was a widow-woman, who had got no husband, because he was dead. Mr. Newberry, he added, had been a well-to-do man enough, as the saying was, and a farmer; but he had gone off in a decline. As regarded Mrs. Newberry's serious side, Stockdale gathered that she was one of the trimmers who went to church and chapel both.

"I'll go there," said Stockdale, feeling that, in the absence of purely sectarian lodgings, he could do no better.

"She's a little particular, and won't hae gover'ment folks, or curates, or the pa'son's friends, or such like," said the lad, dubiously.

"Ah, that may be a promising sign. I'll call. Or no; just you go up and ask first if she can find room for me. I have to see one or two persons on another matter. You will find me down at the carrier's."

In a quarter of an hour the lad came back, and said that Mrs. Newberry would have no objection to accommodate him, whereupon Stockdale called at the house. It stood within a garden hedge, and seemed to be roomy and comfortable. He saw an elderly woman, with whom he made arrangements to come the same night, since there was no inn in the place, and he wished to house himself as soon as possible; the village being a local centre from which he was to radiate at once to the different small chapels in the neighborhood. He forthwith sent his luggage to Mrs. Newberry's from the carrier's, where he had taken shelter, and in the evening walked up to his temporary home.

As he now lived there, Stockdale felt it unnecessary to knock at the door; and entering quietly, he had the pleasure of hearing footsteps scudding away like mice into the back quarters. He advanced to the parlor, as the front room was called, though its stone floor was scarcely disguised by the carpet, which overlaid only the trodden areas, leaving sandy deserts under the furniture. But the room looked snug and cheerful. The firelight shone out brightly, trembling on the bulging mouldings of the table-legs, playing with brass knobs and handles, and lurking in great strength on the under surface of the chimney-piece. A deep arm-chair, covered with horse-hair, and studded with a countless throng of brass nails, was pulled up on one side of the fireplace. The tea-things were on the table, the teapot cover was open, and a little hand-bell had been laid at that precise point towards which a person seated in the great chair might be expected instinctively to stretch his hand.

Stockdale sat down, not objecting to his experience of the room thus far, and began his residence by tinkling the bell. A little girl crept in at the summons, and made tea for him. Her name, she said, was Marther Sarer, and she lived out there, nodding towards the road and village generally. Before Stockdale had got far with his meal a tap sounded on the door behind him, and on his telling the inquirer to come in, a rustle of garments caused him to turn his head. He saw before him a fine and extremely well-made young woman, with dark hair, a wide, sensible, beautiful forehead, eyes that warmed him before he knew it, and a mouth that was in itself a picture to all appreciative souls.

"Can I get you anything else for tea?" she said, coming forward a step or two, an expression of liveliness on her features, and her hand waving the door by its edge.

"Nothing, thank you," said Stockdale, thinking less of what he replied than of what might be her relation to the household.

"You are quite sure?" said the young woman, apparently aware that he had not considered his answer.

He conscientiously examined the tea-things, and found them all there. "Quite sure, Miss Newberry," he said.

"It is Mrs. Newberry," said she. "Lizzy Newberry. I used to be Lizzy Simpkins."

"Oh, I beg your pardon, Mrs. Newberry." And before he had occasion to say more she left the room.

Stockdale remained in some doubt till Martha Sarah came to clear the table. "Whose house is this, my little woman," said he.

"Mrs. Lizzy Newberry's, sir."

"Then Mrs. Newberry is not the old lady I saw this afternoon?"

"No. That's Mrs. Newberry's mother. It was Mrs. Newberry who comed in to you just by now, because she wanted to see if you was good-looking."

Later in the evening, when Stockdale was about to begin supper, she came again. "I have come myself, Mr. Stockdale," she said. The minister stood up in acknowledgment of the honor. "I am afraid little Marther might not make you understand. What will you have for supper? There's cold rabbit, and there's a ham uncut."

Stockdale said he could get on nicely with those viands, and supper was laid. He had no more than cut a slice when tap-tap came to the door again. The minister had already learned that this particular rhythm in taps denoted the fingers of his enkindling landlady, and the doomed young fellow buried his first mouthful under a look of receptive blandness.

"We have a chicken in the house, Mr. Stockdale; I quite forgot to mention it just now. Perhaps you would like Marther Sarer to bring it up?"

Stockdale had advanced far enough in the art of being a young man to say that he did not want the chicken, unless she brought it up herself; but when it was uttered he blushed at the daring gallantry of the speech, perhaps a shade too strong for a serious man and a minister. In three minutes the chicken appeared, but, to his great surprise, only in the hands of Martha Sarah. Stockdale was disappointed, which perhaps it was intended that he should be.

He had finished supper, and was not in the least anticipating Mrs. Newberry again that night, when she tapped and entered as before. Stockdale's gratified look told that she had lost nothing by not appearing when expected. It happened that the cold in the head from which the young man suffered had increased with the approach of night, and before she had spoken he was seized with a violent fit of sneezing, which he could not anyhow repress.

Mrs. Newberry looked full of pity. "Your cold is very bad to-night, Mr. Stockdale."

Stockdale replied that it was rather troublesome.

"And I've a good mind—" she added, archly, looking at the cheerless glass of water on the table, which the abstemious young minister was going to drink.

"Yes, Mrs. Newberry?"

"I've a good mind that you should have something more likely to cure it than that cold stuff."

"Well," said Stockdale, looking down at the glass, "as there is no inn here, and nothing better to be got in the village, of course it will do."

To this she replied, "There is something better, not far off, though not in the house. I really think you must try it, or you may be ill. Yes, Mr. Stockdale, you shall." She held up her finger, seeing that he was about to speak. "Don't ask what it is; wait, and you shall see."

Lizzy went away, and Stockdale waited in a pleasant mood. Presently she returned with her bonnet and cloak on, saying, "I am so sorry, but you must help me to get it. Mother has gone to bed. Will you wrap yourself up, and come this way, and please bring that cup with you?"

Stockdale, a lonely young fellow, who had for weeks felt a great craving for somebody on whom to throw away superfluous interest, and even tenderness, was not sorry to join her, and followed his guide through the back door, across the garden to the bottom, where the boundary was a wall. This wall was low, and beyond it

Stockdale discerned in the night-shades several gray headstones, and the outlines of the church roof or tower.

"It is easy to get up this way," she said, stepping upon a bank which abutted on the wall; then putting her foot on the top of the stone-work, and descending by a spring inside, where the ground was much higher, as is the manner of grave-yards to be. Stockdale did the same, and followed her in the dusk across the irregular ground till they came to the tower door, which, when they had entered, she softly closed behind them.

"You can keep a secret?" she said, in a musical voice.

"Like an iron chest!" said he, fervently.

Then from under her cloak she produced a small lighted lantern, which the minister had not noticed that she carried at all. The light showed them to be close to the singing-gallery stairs, under which lay a heap of lumber of all sorts, but consisting mostly of decayed framework, pews, panels, and pieces of flooring, that from time to time had been removed from their original fixings in the body of the edifice and replaced by new.

"Perhaps you will drag some of those boards aside?" she said, holding the lantern over her head to light him better. "Or will you take the lantern while I move them?"

"I can manage it," said the young man; and acting as she ordered, he uncovered, to his surprise, a row of little barrels bound with wood hoops, each barrel being about as large as the nave of a common wagon-wheel. When they were laid open Lizzy fixed her eyes on him, as if she wondered what he would say.

"You know what they are?" she asked, finding that he did not speak.

"Yes, barrels," said Stockdale simply. He was an inland man, the son of highly respectable parents, and brought up with a single eye to the ministry, and the sight suggested nothing beyond the fact that such articles were there.

"You are quite right; they are barrels," she said, in an emphatic tone of candor that was not without a touch of irony.

Stockdale looked at her with an eye of sudden misgiving. "Not smugglers' liquor?" he said.

"Yes," said she. "They are tubs of spirit that have accidentally come over in the dark from France."

In Nether-Moynton and its vicinity at this date people always smiled at the sort of sin called in the outside world illicit trading,; and these little tubskegs of gin and brandy were as well known to the inhabitants as turnips. So that Stockdale's innocent ignorance, and his look of alarm when he guessed the sinister mystery, seemed to strike Lizzy first as ludicrous, and then as very awkward for the good impression that she wished to produce upon him.

"Smuggling is carried on here by some of the people," she said, in a gentle, apologetic voice. "It has been their practice for generations, and they think it no harm. Now, will you roll out one of the tubs?"

"What to do with it?" said the minister.

"To draw a little from it to cure your cold," she answered. "It is so burning strong that it drives away that sort of thing in a jiffy. Oh, it is all right about our taking it. I may have what I like; the owner of the tubs says so. I ought to have had some in the house, and then I shouldn't ha' been put to this trouble; but I drink none myself, and so I often forget to keep it in-doors."

"You are allowed to help yourself, I suppose, that you may not inform where their hiding-place is?"

"Well, no, not that particularly, but I may take some if I want it. So help yourself."

"I will, to oblige you, since you have a right to it," murmured the minister; and though he was not quite satisfied with his part in the performance, he rolled one of the tubs out from the corner into the middle of the tower floor. "How do you wish me to get it out—with a gimlet, I suppose?"

"No; I'll show you," said his interesting companion. And she held up with her other hand a shoemaker's awl and a hammer. "You must never do these things with a gimlet, because the wood-dust gets in; and when the buyers pour out the brandy, that would tell them that the tub had been broached. An awl makes no dust, and the hole nearly closes up again. Now tap one of the hoops forward."

Stockdale took the hammer and did so.

"Now make the hole in the part that was covered by the hoop."

He made the hole as directed. "It won't run out," he said.

"Oh yes it will," said she. "Take the tub between your knees and squeeze the heads, and I'll hold the cup."

Stockdale obeyed; and the pressure taking effect upon the tub, which seemed to be thin, the spirits spurted out in a stream. When the cup was full he ceased pressing, and the flow immediately stopped. "Now we must fill up the keg with water," said Lizzy, "or it will cluck like forty hens when it is handled, and show that 'tis not full."

"But they tell you you may take it?"

"Yes, the *smugglers;* but the *buyers* must not know that the smugglers have been kind to me at their expense."

"I see," said Stockdale, doubtfully. "I much question the honesty of this proceeding."

By her direction he held the tub with the hole upward, and while he went through the process of alternately pressing and ceasing to press she produced a bottle of water, from which she took mouthfuls, then putting her pretty lips to the hole, where it was sucked in at each recovery of the cask from pressure. When it was again full he plugged the hole, knocked the hoop down to its place, and buried the tub in the lumber as before.

"Aren't the smugglers afraid that you will tell?" he asked as they recrossed the church-yard.

"Oh no; they are not afraid of that. I couldn't do such a thing."

"They have put you into a very awkward corner," said Stockdale, emphatically. "You must, of course, as an honest person, sometimes feel that it is your duty to inform—really, you must."

"Well, I have never particularly felt it as a duty; and, besides, my first husband—" She stopped, and there was some confusion in her voice. Stockdale was so honest and unsophisticated that he did not at once discern why she paused; but at last he did perceive that the words were a slip, and that no woman would have uttered "first husband" by accident unless she had thought pretty frequently of a second. He felt for her confusion, and allowed her time to recover and proceed. "My husband," she said, in a self-corrected tone, "used to know of their doings, and so did my father, and kept the secret. I cannot inform, in fact, against anybody."

"I see the hardness of it," he continued, like a man

who looked far into the moral of things. "And it is very cruel that you should be tossed and tantalized between your memories and your conscience. I do hope, Mrs. Newberry, that you will soon see your way out of this unpleasant position."

"Well, I don't just now," she murmured.

By this time they had passed over the wall and entered the house, where she brought him a glass and hot water, and left him to his own reflections. He looked after her vanishing form, asking himself whether he, as a respectable man, and a minister, and a shining light, even though as yet only of the halfpenny-candle sort, were quite justified in doing this thing. A sneeze settled the question; and he found that when the fiery liquor was lowered by the addition of twice or thrice the quantity of water, it was one of the prettiest cures for a cold in the head that he had ever known, particularly at this chilly time of the year.

Stockdale sat in the deep chair about twenty minutes sipping and meditating, till he at length took warmer views of things, and longed for the morrow, when he would see Mrs. Newberry again. He then felt that, though chronologically at a short distance, it would, in an emotional sense, be very long before to-morrow came, and walked restlessly round the room. His eye was attracted by a framed and glazed sampler in which a running ornament of fir-trees and peacocks surrounded the following pretty bit of sentiment:

> "Rose-leaves smell when roses thrive,
> Here's my work while I'm alive;
> Rose-leaves smell when shrunk and shed,
> Here's my work when I am dead.

> "Lizzy Simpkins. Fear God. Honor the King. Aged 11 years."

"'Tis hers," he said to himself. "Heavens, how I like that name!"

Before he had done thinking that no other name from Abigail to Zenobia would have suited his young landlady so well, tap-tap came again upon the door; and the minister started as her face appeared yet another time, looking so disinterested that the most ingenious would have refrained from asserting that she had come to affect his feelings by her seductive eyes.

"Would you like a fire in your room, Mr. Stockdale, on account of your cold?"

The minister, being still a little pricked in the conscience for countenancing her in watering the spirits, saw here a way to self-chastisement. "No, I thank you," he said firmly; "it is not necessary. I have never been used to one in my life, and it would be giving way to luxury too far."

"Then I won't insist," she said, and disconcerted him by vanishing instantly.

Wondering if she was vexed by his refusal, he wished that he had chosen to have a fire, even though it should have scorched him out of bed and endangered his self-discipline for a dozen days. However, he consoled himself with what was in truth a rare consolation for a budding lover, that he was under the same roof with Lizzy—her guest, in fact, to take a poetical view of the term lodger; and that he would certainly see her on the morrow.

The morrow came, and Stockdale rose early, his cold quite gone. He had never in his life so longed for the breakfast-hour as he did that day, and punctually at eight o'clock, after a short walk, to reconnoitre the premises, he re-entered the door of his dwelling. Breakfast passed, and Martha Sarah attended, but nobody came voluntarily as on the night before to inquire if there were other wants which he had not mentioned, and which she would attempt to gratify. He was disappointed, and went out, hoping to see her at dinner. Dinner-time came; he sat down to the meal, finished it, lingered on for a whole hour, although two new teachers were at that moment waiting at the chapel door to speak to him by appointment. It was useless to wait longer, and he slowly went his way down the lane, cheered by the thought that, after all, he would see her in the evening, and perhaps engage again in the delightful tub-broaching in the neighboring church tower, which proceeding he resolved to render more moral by steadfastly insisting that no water should be introduced to fill up, though the tub should cluck like all the hens in Christendom. But nothing could disguise the fact that it was a queer business; and his countenance fell when he thought how much more his mind was interested in that matter than in his serious duties.

However, compunction vanished with the decline of day. Night came, and his tea and supper; but no Lizzy Newberry, and no sweet temptations. At last the minister could bear it no longer, and said to his quaint little attendant, "Where is Mrs. Newberry to-day?" judiciously handing a penny as he spoke.

"She's busy," said Martha.

"Anything serious happened?" he asked, handing another penny, and revealing yet additional pennies in the background.

"Oh no, nothing at all!" said she, with breathless confidence. "Nothing ever happens to her. She's only biding up-stairs in bed, because 'tis her way sometimes."

Being a young man of some honor, he would not question further, and assuming that Lizzy must have a bad headache, or other slight ailment, in spite of what the girl had said, he went to bed dissatisfied, not even setting eyes on old Mrs. Simpkins. "I said last night that I should see her to-morrow," he reflected; "but that was not to be!"

Next day he had better fortune, or worse, meeting her at the foot of the stairs in the morning, and being favored by a visit or two from her during the day—once for the purpose of making kindly inquiries about his comfort, as on the first evening, and at another time to place a bunch of winter-violets on his table, with a promise to renew them when they drooped. On these occasions there was something in her smile which showed how conscious she was of the effect she produced, though it must be said that it was rather a humorous than a designing consciousness, and savored more of pride than of vanity.

As for Stockdale, he clearly perceived that he possessed unlimited capacity for backsliding, and wished that tutelary saints were not denied to Dissenters. He set a watch upon his tongue and eyes for the space of one hour and a half, after which he found it was useless to struggle further, and gave himself up to the situation. "The other minister will be here in a month," he said to himself when sitting over the fire. "Then I shall be off, and she will distract my mind no more!... And then, shall I go on living by myself forever? No; when my two years of probation are finished, I shall have a furnished house to live in, with a varnished door and a brass knocker; and I'll march straight back to her, and ask her flat, as soon as the last plate is on the dresser!"

Thus a titillating fortnight was passed by young Stockdale, during which time things proceeded much as such matters have done ever since the beginning of history. He saw the object of attachment several times one day, did not see her at all the next, met her when he least expected to do so, missed her when hints and signs as to where she should be at a given hour almost amounted to an appointment. This mild coquetry was perhaps fair enough under the circumstances of their being so closely lodged, and Stockdale put up with it as philosophically as he was able. Being in her own house, she could, after vexing or disappointing him of her presence, easily win him back by suddenly surrounding him with those little attentions which her position as his landlady put it in her power to bestow. When he had waited in-doors half the day to see her, and on finding that she would not be seen, had gone off in a huff to the dreariest and dampest walk he could discover, she would restore equilibrium in the evening with "Mr. Stockdale, I have fancied you must feel draught o' nights from your bedroom window, and so I have been putting up thicker curtains this afternoon while you were out;" or "I noticed that you sneezed twice again this morning, Mr. Stockdale. Depend upon it, that

CHAPTER II
HOW HE SAW TWO OTHER MEN

Matters being in this advanced state, Stockdale was rather surprised one cloudy evening, while sitting in his room, at hearing her speak in low tones of expostulation to some one at the door. It was nearly dark, but the shutters were not yet closed, nor the candles lighted; and Stockdale was tempted to stretch his head towards the window. He saw outside the door a young man in clothes of a whitish color, and upon reflection judged their wearer to be the well-built and rather handsome miller who lived below. The miller's voice was alternately low and firm, and sometimes it reached the level of positive entreaty; but what the words were Stockdale could in no way hear.

Before the colloquy had ended, the minister's attention was attracted by a second incident. Opposite Lizzy's home grew a clump of laurels, forming a thick and permanent shade. One of the laurel boughs now quivered against the light background of sky, and in a moment the head of a man peered out, and remained still. He seemed to be also much interested in the conversation at the door, and was plainly lingering there to watch and listen. Had Stockdale stood in any other relation to Lizzy than that of a lover, he might have gone out and investigated the meaning of this; but being as yet but an unprivileged ally, he did nothing more than stand up and show himself in the lighted room, whereupon the listener disappeared, and Lizzy and the miller spoke in lower tones.

Stockdale was made so uneasy by the circumstance that as soon as the miller was gone, he said, "Mrs. Newberry, are you aware that you were watched just now, and your conversation heard?"

"When?" she said.

"When you were talking to that miller. A man was looking from the laurel-tree as jealously as if he could have eaten you."

She showed more concern than the trifling event seemed to demand, and he added, "Perhaps you were talking of things you did not wish to be overheard?"

"I was talking only on business," she said.

"Lizzy, be frank!" said the young man. "If it was only on business, why should anybody wish to listen to you?"

She looked curiously at him. "What else do you think it could be, then?"

"Well, the only talk between a young woman and man that is likely to amuse an eavesdropper."

"Ah yes," she said, smiling in spite of her preoccupation. "Well, Cousin Owlett has spoken to me about matrimony, every now and then, that's true; but he was not speaking of it then. I wish he had been speaking of it, with all my heart. It would have been much less serious for me."

"Oh, Mrs. Newberry!"

"It would. Not that I should ha' chimed in with him, of course. I wish it for other reasons. I am glad, Mr. Stockdale, that you have told me of that listener. It is a timely warning, and I must see my cousin again."

"But don't go away till I have spoken," said the minister. "I'll out with it at once, and make no more ado. Let it be Yes or No between us, Lizzy, please do!" And he held out his hand, in which she freely allowed her own to rest, but without speaking.

"You mean Yes by that?" he asked, after waiting a while.

"You may be my sweetheart, if you will."

"Why not say at once you will wait for me until I have a house and can come back to marry you?"

"Because I am thinking—thinking of something

else," she said with embarrassment. "It all comes upon me at once, and I must settle one thing at a time."

"At any rate, dear Lizzy, you can assure me that the miller shall not be allowed to speak to you except on business? You have never directly encouraged him?"

She parried the question by saying, "You see, he and his party have been in the habit of leaving things on my premises sometimes, and as I have not denied him, it makes him rather forward."

"Things—what things?"

"Tubs—they are called things here."

"But why don't you deny him, my dear Lizzy?"

"I cannot well."

"You are too timid. It is unfair of him to impose so upon you, and get your good name into danger by his smuggling tricks. Promise me that the next time he wants to leave his tubs here you will let me roll them into the street?"

She shook her head. "I would not venture to offend the neighbors so much as that," said she, "or do anything that would be so likely to put poor Owlett into the hands of the excisemen."

Stockdale sighed, and said that he thought hers a mistaken generosity when it extended to assisting those who cheated the King of his dues. "At any rate, you will let me make him keep his distance as your lover, and tell him flatly that you are not for him?"

"Please not, at present," she said. "I don't wish to offend my old neighbors. It is not only Owlett who is concerned."

"This is too bad," said Stockdale, impatiently.

"On my honor, I won't encourage him as my lover," Lizzy answered earnestly. "A reasonable man will be satisfied with that."

"Well, so I am," said Stockdale, his countenance clearing.

CHAPTER III
THE MYSTERIOUS GREAT-COAT

Stockdale now began to notice more particularly a fea-
ture in the life of his fair landlady which he had casually
observed, but scarcely ever thought of before. It was that
she was markedly irregular in her hours of rising. For
a week or two she would be tolerably punctual, reaching the ground-floor within a few minutes of half-past
seven; then suddenly she would not be visible till twelve
at noon, perhaps for three or four days in succession;
and twice he had certain proof that she did not leave her
room till half-past three in the afternoon. The second
time that this extreme lateness came under his notice
was on a day when he had particularly wished to consult
with her about his future movements; and he concluded,
as he always had done, that she had a cold, headache,
or other ailment, unless she had kept herself invisible
to avoid meeting and talking to him, which he could

hardly believe. The former supposition was disproved, however, by her innocently saying, some days later, when they were speaking on a question of health, that she had never had a moment's heaviness, headache, or illness of any kind since the previous January twelvemonth.

"I am glad to hear it," said he. "I thought quite otherwise."

"What, do I look sickly?" she asked, turning up her face to show the impossibility of his gazing on it and holding such a belief for a moment.

"Not at all; I merely thought so from your being sometimes obliged to keep your room through the best part of the day."

"Oh, as for that—it means nothing," she murmured, with a look which some might have called cold, and which was the look that he worst liked to see upon her. "It is pure sleepiness, Mr. Stockdale."

"Never!"

"It is, I tell you. When I stay in my room till half-past three in the afternoon, you may always be sure that I slept soundly till three, or I shouldn't have stayed there."

"It is dreadful," said Stockdale, thinking of the disastrous effects of such indulgence upon the household of a minister, should it become a habit of every-day occurrence.

"But then," she said, divining his good and prescient

thoughts, "it only happens when I stay awake all night. I don't go to sleep till five or six in the morning sometimes."

"Ah, that's another matter," said Stockdale. "Sleeplessness to such an alarming extent is real illness. Have you spoken to a doctor?"

"Oh no, there is no need for doing that; it is all natural to me." And she went away without further remark.

Stockdale might have waited a long time to know the real cause of her sleeplessness, had it not happened that one dark night he was sitting in his bedroom jotting down notes for a sermon, which unintentionally occupied him for a considerable time after the other members of the household had retired. He did not get to bed till one o'clock. Before he had fallen asleep he heard a knocking at the front door, first rather timidly performed, and then louder. Nobody answered it, and the person knocked again. As the house still remained undisturbed, Stockdale got out of bed, went to his window, which overlooked the door, and opening it, asked who was there.

A young woman's voice replied that Susan Wallis was there, and that she had come to ask if Mrs. Newberry could give her some mustard to make a plaster with, as her father was taken very ill on the chest.

The minister, having neither bell nor servant, was compelled to act in person. "I will call Mrs. Newberry," he said. Partly dressing himself, he went along the passage and tapped at Lizzy's door. She did not answer, and, thinking of her erratic habits in the matter of sleep, he thumped the door persistently, when he discovered, by its moving ajar under his knocking, that it had only been gently pushed to. As there was now a sufficient entry for the voice, he knocked no longer, but said in firm tones, "Mrs. Newberry, you are wanted."

The room was quite silent; not a breathing, not a rustle, came from any part of it. Stockdale now sent a positive shout through the open space of the door: "Mrs. Newberry!" still no answer, or movement of any kind within. Then he heard sounds from the opposite room, that of Lizzy's mother, as if she had been aroused by his uproar though Lizzy had not, and was dressing herself hastily. Stockdale softly closed the younger woman's door and went on to the other, which was opened by Mrs. Simpkins before he could reach it. She was in her ordinary clothes, and had a light in her hand.

"What's the person calling about?" she said, in alarm.

Stockdale told the girl's errand, adding seriously, "I cannot wake Mrs. Newberry."

"It is no matter," said her mother. "I can let the girl have what she wants as well as my daughter." And she came out of the room and went down-stairs.

Stockdale retired towards his own apartment, saying,

however, to Mrs. Simpkins from the landing, as if on second thoughts, "I suppose there is nothing the matter with Mrs. Newberry, that I could not wake her?"

"Oh no," said the old lady, hastily. "Nothing at all."

Still the minister was not satisfied. "Will you go in and see?" he said. "I should be much more at ease."

Mrs. Simpkins returned up the staircase, went to her daughter's room, and came out again almost instantly. "There is nothing at all the matter with Lizzy," she said, and descended again to attend to the applicant, who, having seen the light, had remained quiet during this interval.

Stockdale went into his room and lay down as before. He heard Lizzy's mother open the front door, admit the girl, and then the murmured discourse of both as they went to the store-cupboard for the medicament required. The girl departed, the door was fastened, Mrs. Simpkins came up-stairs, and the house was again in silence. Still the minister did not fall asleep. He could not get rid of a singular suspicion, which was all the more harassing in being, if true, the most unaccountable thing within his experience. That Lizzy Newberry was in her bedroom when he made such a clamor at her door he could not possibly convince himself, notwithstanding that he had heard her come up-stairs at the usual time, go into her chamber, and shut herself up in the usual way. Yet all reason was so much against her being elsewhere that he was constrained to go back again to the unlikely theory of a heavy sleep, though he had heard neither breath nor movement during a shouting and knocking loud enough to rouse the Seven Sleepers.

Before coming to any positive conclusion he fell asleep himself, and did not awake till day. He saw nothing of Mrs. Newberry in the morning, before he went out to meet the rising sun, as he liked to do when the weather was fine; but as this was by no means unusual, he took no notice of it. At breakfast-time he knew that she was not far off by hearing her in the kitchen, and though he saw nothing of her person, that back apartment being rigorously closed against his eyes, she seemed to be talking, ordering, and bustling about among the pots and skimmers in so ordinary a manner that there was no reason for his wasting more time in fruitless surmise.

The minister suffered from these distractions, and his extemporized sermons were not improved thereby. Already he often said Romans for Corinthians in the pulpit, and gave out hymns in strange cramped metres that hitherto had always been skipped because the congregation could not raise a tune to fit them. He fully resolved that as soon as his few weeks of stay approached their end he would cut the matter short, and commit himself by proposing a definite engagement, repenting at leisure if necessary.

With this end in view, he suggested to her on the evening after her mysterious sleep that they should take a walk together just before dark, the latter part of the proposition being introduced that they might return home unseen. She consented to go; and away they went over a stile, to a shrouded foot-path suited for the occasion. But, in spite of attempts on both sides, they were unable to infuse much spirit into the ramble. She looked rather paler than usual, and sometimes turned her head away.

"Lizzy," said Stockdale, reproachfully, when they had walked in silence a long distance.

"Yes," said she.

"You yawned—much my company is to you!" He put it in that way, but he was really wondering whether her yawn could possibly have more to do with physical weariness from the night before than mental weariness of that present moment. Lizzy apologized, and owned that she was rather tired, which gave him an opening for a direct question on the point; but his modesty would not allow him to put it to her, and he uncomfortably resolved to wait.

The month of February passed with alternations of mud and frost, rain and sleet, east winds and north-westerly gales. The hollow places in the ploughed fields showed themselves as pools of water, which had settled there from the higher levels, and had not yet found time to soak away. The birds began to get lively, and a single thrush came just before sunset each evening, and sang hopefully on the large elm-tree which stood nearest to Mrs. Newberry's house. Cold blasts and brittle earth had given place to an oozing dampness more unpleasant in itself than frost; but it suggested coming spring, and its unpleasantness was of a bearable kind.

Stockdale had been going to bring about a practical understanding with Lizzy at least half a dozen times; but what with the mystery of her apparent absence on the night of the neighbor's call, and her curious way of lying in bed at unaccountable times, he felt a check within him whenever he wanted to speak out. Thus they still lived on as indefinitely affianced lovers, each of whom hardly acknowledged the other's claim to the name of chosen one. Stockdale persuaded himself that his hesitation was owing to the postponement of the ordained minister's arrival, and the consequent delay in his own departure, which did away with all necessity for haste in his courtship; but perhaps it was only that his discretion was reasserting itself, and telling him that he had better get clearer ideas of Lizzy before arranging for the grand contract of his life with her. She, on her part, always

a tone of confusion. "Why, Marther Sarer, I did not tell you to take 'em to Mr. Stockdale's room?"

"I thought they must be his as they was so muddy," said Martha, humbly.

"You should have left 'em on the clothes-horse," said the young mistress, severely; and she came up-stairs with the garments on her arm, quickly passed Stockdale's room, and threw them forcibly into a closet at the end of a passage. With this the incident ended, and the house was silent again.

There would have been nothing remarkable in finding such clothes in a widow's house had they been clean, or moth-eaten, or creased, or mouldy from long lying by; but that they should be splashed with recent mud bothered Stockdale a good deal. When a young pastor is in the aspen stage of attachment, and open to agitation at the merest trifles, a really substantial incongruity of this complexion is a disturbing thing. However, nothing further occurred at that time; but he became watchful and given to conjecture, and was unable to forget the circumstance.

One morning, on looking from his window, he saw Mrs. Newberry herself brushing the tails of a long drab great-coat, which, if he mistook not, was the very same garment as the one that had adorned the chair of his room. It was densely splashed up to the hollow of the back with neighboring Nether-Moynton mud, to judge by its color, the spots being distinctly visible to him in the sunlight. The previous day or two having been wet, the inference was irresistible that the wearer had quite recently been walking some considerable distance about the lanes and fields. Stockdale opened the window and looked out, and Mrs. Newberry turned her head. Her face became slowly red; she never had looked prettier, or more incomprehensible. He waved his hand affectionately, and said good-morning; she answered with embarrassment, having ceased her occupation on the instant that she saw him, and rolled up the coat half cleaned.

Stockdale shut the window. Some simple explanation of her proceeding was doubtless within the bounds of possibility; but he himself could not think of one; and he wished that she had placed the matter beyond conjecture by voluntarily saying something about it there and then.

But, though Lizzy had not offered an explanation at the moment, the subject was brought forward by her at the next time of their meeting. She was chatting to him concerning some other event, and remarked that it happened about the time when she was dusting some old clothes that had belonged to her poor husband.

"You keep them clean out of respect to his memory?" said Stockdale, tentatively.

"I air and dust them sometimes," she said, with the most charming innocence in the world.

"Do dead men come out of their graves and walk in mud?" murmured the minister, in a cold sweat at the deception that she was practising.

"What did you say?" asked Lizzy.

"Nothing, nothing," said he, mournfully. "Mere words—a phrase that will do for my sermon next Sunday." It was too plain that Lizzy was unaware that he had seen actual pedestrian splashes upon the skirts of the telltale overcoat, and that she imagined him to believe it had come direct from some chest or drawer.

The aspect of the case was now considerably darker. Stockdale was so much depressed by it that he did not challenge her explanation, or threaten to go off as a missionary to benighted islanders, or reproach her in any way whatever. He simply parted from her when she had done talking, and lived on in perplexity, till by degrees his natural manner became sad and constrained.

CHAPTER IV
AT THE TIME OF THE NEW MOON

The following Thursday was changeable, damp, and gloomy, and the night threatened to be windy and unpleasant. Stockdale had gone away to Knollsea in the morning, to be present at some commemoration service there, and on his return he was met by the attractive Lizzy in the passage. Whether influenced by the tide of cheerfulness which had attended him that day, or by the drive through the open air, or whether from a natural disposition to let by-gones alone, he allowed himself to be fascinated into forgetfulness of the great-coat incident, and, upon the whole, passed a pleasant evening; not so much in her society as within sound of her voice, as she sat talking in the back parlor to her mother, till the latter went to bed. Shortly after this Mrs. Newberry retired, and then Stockdale prepared to go up-stairs himself. But before he left the room he remained standing by the dying embers a while, thinking long of one thing and another, and was only aroused by the flickering of his candle in the socket as it suddenly declined and went out. Knowing that there were a tinder-box, matches, and another candle in his bedroom, he felt his way up-stairs without a light. On reaching his chamber he laid his hand on every possible ledge and corner for the tinder-box, but for a long time in vain. Discovering it at length, Stockdale produced a spark, and was kindling the brimstone, when he fancied that he heard a movement in the passage. He blew harder at the lint, the match flared up, and looking by aid of the blue light through the door, which had been standing open all this time, he was surprised to see a male figure vanishing round the top of the staircase with the evident intention of escaping unobserved. The personage wore the clothes which Lizzy had been brushing, and something in the outline and gait suggested to the minister that the wearer was Lizzy herself.

But he was not sure of this; and, greatly excited, Stockdale determined to investigate the mystery, and to adopt his own way for doing it. He blew out the match without lighting the candle, went into the passage, and proceeded on tiptoe towards Lizzy's room. A faint gray square of light in the direction of the chamber window as he approached told him that the door was open, and at once suggested that the occupant was gone. He turned and brought down his fist upon the hand-rail of the staircase: "It was she; in her late husband's coat and hat!"

Somewhat relieved to find that there was no intruder in the case, yet none the less surprised, the minister crept down the stairs, softly put on his boots, overcoat, and hat, and tried the front door. It was fastened as usual; he went to the back door, found this unlocked, and emerged into the garden. The night was mild and moonless, and rain had lately been falling, though for the present it had ceased. There was a sudden dropping from the trees and bushes every now and then, as each passing wind shook their boughs. Among these sounds Stockdale heard the faint fall of feet upon the road outside, and he guessed from the step that it was Lizzy's. He followed the sound, and, helped by the circumstance of the wind blowing from the direction in which the pedestrian moved, he got nearly close to her, and kept there, without risk of being overheard. While he thus followed her up the street or lane, as it might indifferently be called, there being more hedge than houses on either side, a figure came forward to her from one of the cottage doors. Lizzy stopped; the minister stepped upon the grass and stopped also.

"Is that Mrs. Newberry?" said the man who had come out, whose voice Stockdale recognized as that of one of the most devout members of his congregation.

"It is," said Lizzy.

"I be quite ready—I've been here this quarter-hour."

"Ah, John," said she, "I have bad news; there is danger to-night for our venture."

"And d'ye tell o't! I dreamed there might be."

"Yes," she said, hurriedly; "and you must go at once round to where the chaps are waiting, and tell them they will not be wanted till to-morrow night at the same time. I go to burn the lugger off."

"I will," he said, and instantly went off through a gate, Lizzy continuing her way.

On she tripped at a quickening pace till the lane turned into the turnpike-road, which she crossed, and got into the track for Ringsworth. Here she ascended the hill without the least hesitation, passed the lonely hamlet of Holworth, and went down the vale on the other side. Stockdale had never taken any extensive walks in this direction, but he was aware that if she persisted in her course much longer she would draw near to the coast, which was here between two and three miles distant from Nether-Moynton; and as it had been about a quarter-past eleven o'clock when they set out, her intention seemed to be to reach the shore about midnight.

Lizzy soon ascended a small mound, which Stockdale at the same time adroitly skirted on the left; and a dull monotonous roar burst upon his ear. The hillock was about fifty yards from the top of the cliffs, and by day it apparently commanded a full view of the bay. There was light enough in the sky to show her disguised figure against it when she reached the top, where she paused, and afterwards sat down. Stockdale, not wishing on any account to alarm her at this moment, yet desirous of being near her, sank upon his hands and knees, crept a little higher up, and there stayed still.

The wind was chilly, the ground damp, and his position one in which he did not care to remain long. However, before he had decided to leave it, the young man heard voices behind him. What they signified he did not know; but, fearing that Lizzy was in danger, he was about to run forward and warn her that she might be seen, when she crept to the shelter of a little bush which maintained a precarious existence in that exposed spot; and her form was absorbed in its dark and stunted outline as if she had become part of it. She had evidently heard the men as well as he. They passed near him, talking in loud and careless tones, which could be heard above the uninterrupted washings of the sea, and which suggested that they were not engaged in any business at their own risk. This proved to be the fact; some of their words floated across to him, and caused him to forget at once the coldness of his situation.

"What's the vessel?"

"A lugger, about fifty tons."

"From Cherbourg, I suppose?"

"Yes, a b'lieve."

"But it don't all belong to Owlett?"

"Oh no. He's only got a share. There's another or two in it—a farmer and such-like, but the names I don't know."

The voices died away, and the heads and shoulders of the men diminished towards the cliff, and dropped out of sight.

"My darling has been tempted to buy a share by that unbeliever Owlett," groaned the minister, his honest affection for Lizzy having quickened to its intensest point during these moments of risk to her person and name. "That's why she's here," he said to himself. "Oh, it will be the ruin of her!"

His perturbation was interrupted by the sudden bursting out of a bright and increasing light from the spot where Lizzy was in hiding. A few seconds later, and before it had reached the height of a blaze, he heard her rush past him down the hollow like a stone from a sling, in the direction of home. The light now flared high and wide, and showed its position clearly. She had kindled a bough of furze and stuck it into the bush under which she had been crouching; the wind fanned the flame, which crackled fiercely, and threatened to consume the bush as well as the bough. Stockdale paused just long enough to notice thus much, and then followed rapidly the route taken by the young woman. His intention was to overtake her, and reveal himself as a friend; but run as he would he could see nothing of her. Thus he flew across the open country about Holworth, twisting his legs and ankles in unexpected fissures and descents, till, on coming to the gate between the downs and the road, he was forced to pause to get breath. There was no audible movement either in front or behind him, and he now concluded that she had not outrun him, but that, hearing him at her heels, and believing him one of the excise party, she had hidden herself somewhere on the way, and let him pass by.

He went on at a more leisurely pace towards the village. On reaching the house he found his surmise to be correct, for the gate was on the latch, and the door unfastened, just as he had left them. Stockdale closed the door behind him, and waited silently in the passage. In about ten minutes he heard the same light footstep that he had heard in going out; it paused at the gate, which opened and shut softly, and then the door-latch was lifted, and Lizzy came in.

Stockdale went forward and said at once, "Lizzy, don't be frightened. I have been waiting up for you."

She started, though she had recognized the voice. "It is Mr. Stockdale, isn't it?" she said.

"Yes," he answered, becoming angry now that she was safe in-doors, and not alarmed. "And a nice game I've found you out in to-night. You are in man's clothes, and I am ashamed of you!"

Lizzy could hardly find a voice to answer this unexpected reproach.

"I am only partly in man's clothes," she faltered, shrinking back to the wall. "It is only his great-coat and hat and breeches that I've got on, which is no harm, as he was my own husband; and I do it only because a cloak blows about so, and you can't use your arms. I have got my own dress under just the same—it is only tucked in. Will you go away up-stairs and let me pass? I didn't want you to see me at such a time as this."

"But I have a right to see you. How do you think there can be anything between us now?" Lizzy was silent. "You are a smuggler," he continued, sadly.

"I have only a share in the run," she said.

"That makes no difference. Whatever did you engage in such a trade as that for, and keep it such a secret from me all this time?"

"I don't do it always. I do it only in winter-time when 'tis new moon."

"Well, I suppose that's because it can't be done

anywhen else … You have regularly upset me, Lizzy."

"I am sorry for that," Lizzy meekly replied.

"Well now," said he, more tenderly, "no harm is done as yet. Won't you for the sake of me give up this blamable and dangerous practice altogether?"

"I must do my best to save this run," said she, getting rather husky in the throat. "I don't want to give you up—you know that; but I don't want to lose my venture. I don't know what to do now! Why I have kept it so secret from you is that I was afraid you would be angry if you knew."

"I should think so. I suppose if I had married you without finding this out you'd have gone on with it just the same?"

"I don't know. I did not think so far ahead. I only went to-night to burn the folks off, because we found that the excisemen knew where the tubs were to be landed."

"It is a pretty mess to be in altogether, is this," said the distracted young minister. "Well, what will you do now?"

Lizzy slowly murmured the particulars of their plan, the chief of which were that they meant to try their luck at some other point of the shore the next night; that three landing-places were always agreed upon before the run was attempted, with the understanding that, if the vessel was burned off from the first point, which was Ringsworth, as it had been by her to-night, the crew should attempt to make the second, which was Lullstead, on the second night; and if there, too, danger threatened, they should on the third night try the third place, which was behind a headland farther west.

"Suppose the officers hinder them landing there too?" he said, his attention to this interesting programme displacing for a moment his concern at her share in it.

"Then we sha'n't try anywhere else all this dark—that's what we call the time between moon and moon—and perhaps they'll string the tubs to a stray-line, and sink 'em a little ways from shore, and take the bearings; and then when they have a chance they'll go to creep for 'em."

"What's that?"

"Oh, they'll go out in a boat and drag a creeper—that's a grapnel—along the bottom till it catch hold of the stray-line."

The minister stood thinking; and there was no sound within-doors but the tick of the clock on the stairs, and the quick breathing of Lizzy, partly from her walk and partly from agitation, as she stood close to the wall, not in such complete darkness but that he could discern against its whitewashed surface the great-coat and broad hat which covered her.

"Lizzy, all this is very wrong," he said. "Don't you remember the lesson of the tribute-money?—'Render unto Caesar the things that are Caesar's.' Surely you have heard that read times enough in your growing up?"

"He's dead," she pouted.

"But the spirit of the text is in force just the same."

"My father did it, and so did my grandfather, and almost everybody in Nether-Moynton lives by it; and life would be so dull if it wasn't for that, that I should not care to live at all."

"I am nothing to live for, of course," he replied, bitterly. "You would not think it worth while to give up this wild business and live for me alone?"

"I have never looked at it like that."

"And you won't promise and wait till I am ready?"

"I cannot give you my word to-night." And, looking thoughtfully down, she gradually moved and moved away, going into the adjoining room, and closing the door between them. She remained there in the dark till he was tired of waiting, and had gone up to his own chamber.

Poor Stockdale was dreadfully depressed all the next day by the discoveries of the night before. Lizzy was unmistakably a fascinating young woman, but as a minister's wife she was hardly to be contemplated. "If I had only stuck to father's little grocery business, instead of going in for the ministry, she would have suited me beautifully!" he said, sadly, until he remembered that in that case he would never have come from his distant home to Nether-Moynton, and never have known her.

The estrangement between them was not complete, but it was sufficient to keep them out of each other's company. Once during the day he met her in the garden path, and said, turning a reproachful eye upon her, "Do you promise, Lizzy?" But she did not reply. The evening drew on, and he knew well enough that Lizzy would repeat her excursion at night—her half-offended manner had shown that she had not the slightest intention of altering her plans at present. He did not wish to repeat his own share of the adventure; but, act as he would, his uneasiness on her account increased with the decline of day. Supposing that an accident should befall her, he would never forgive himself for not being there to help, much as he disliked the idea of seeming to countenance such unlawful escapades.

CHAPTER V
HOW THEY WENT TO LULLSTEAD COVE AND BACK

As he had expected, she left the house at the same hour at night, this time passing his door without stealth, as if she knew very well that he would be watching, and were resolved to brave his displeasure. He was quite ready, opened the door quickly, and reached the back door almost as soon as she.

"Then you will go, Lizzy?" he said, as he stood on the step beside her, who now again appeared as a little man with a face altogether unsuited to his clothes.

"I must," she said, repressed by his stern manner.

"Then I shall go too," said he.

"And I am sure you will enjoy it!" she exclaimed, in more buoyant tones. "Everybody does who tries it."

"God forbid that I should," he said. "But I must look after you."

They opened the wicket and went up the road

abreast of each other, but at some distance apart, scarcely a word passing between them. The evening was rather less favorable to smuggling enterprise than the last had been, the wind being lower, and the sky somewhat clear towards the north.

"It is rather lighter," said Stockdale.

"'Tis, unfortunately," said she. "But it is only from those few stars over there. The moon was new to-day at four o'clock, and I expected clouds. I hope we shall be able to do it this dark, for when we have to sink 'em for long it makes the stuff taste bleachy, and folks don't like it so well."

Her course was different from that of the preceding night, branching off to the left over Lord's Barrow as soon as they had got out of the lane and crossed the highway. By the time they reached Chaldon Down, Stockdale, who had been in perplexed thought as to what he should say to her, decided that he would not attempt expostulation now, while she was excited by the adventure, but wait till it was over, and endeavor to keep her from such practices in future. It occurred to him once or twice, as they rambled on, that should they be surprised by the excisemen, his situation would be more awkward than hers, for it would be difficult to prove his true motive in coming to the spot; but the risk was a slight consideration beside his wish to be with her.

They now arrived at a ravine which lay on the outskirts of Chaldon, a village two miles on their way towards the point of the shore they sought. Lizzy broke the silence this time: "I have to wait here to meet the carriers. I don't know if they have come yet. As I told you, we go to Lullstead to-night, and it is two miles farther than Ringsworth."

It turned out that the men had already come; for while she spoke two or three dozen heads broke the line of the slope, and a company of men at once descended from the bushes where they had been lying in wait. These carriers were men whom Lizzy and other proprietors regularly employed to bring the tubs from the boat to a hiding-place inland. They were all young fellows of Nether-Moynton, Chaldon, and the neighborhood, quiet and inoffensive persons, who simply engaged to carry the cargo for Lizzy and her cousin Owlett, as they would have engaged in any other labor for which they were fairly well paid.

At a word from her, they closed in together. "You had better take it now," she said to them, and handed to each a packet. It contained six shillings, their remuneration for the night's undertaking, which was paid beforehand without reference to success or failure; but, besides this, they had the privilege of selling as agents when the run was successfully made. As soon as it was done, she said to them, "The place is the old one near Lullstead;" the men till that moment not having been told whither they were bound, for obvious reasons. "Owlett will meet you there," added Lizzy. "I shall follow behind, to see that we are not watched."

The carriers went on, and Stockdale and Mrs. Newberry followed at a distance of a stone's-throw. "What do these men do by day?" he said.

"Twelve or fourteen of them are laboring men. Some are brickmakers, some carpenters, some masons, some thatchers. They are all known to me very well. Nine of 'em are of your own congregation."

"I can't help that," said Stockdale.

"Oh, I know you can't. I only told you. The others are more church-inclined, because they supply the pa'son with all the spirits he requires, and they don't wish to show unfriendliness to a customer."

"How do you choose them?" said Stockdale.

"We choose 'em for their closeness, and because they are strong and sure-footed, and able to carry a heavy load a long way without being tired." Stockdale sighed as she enumerated each particular, for it proved how far involved in the business a woman must be who was so well acquainted with its conditions and needs. And yet he felt more tenderly towards her at this moment than he had felt all the foregoing day. Perhaps it was that her experienced manner and hold indifference stirred his admiration in spite of himself.

"Take my arm, Lizzy," he murmured.

"I don't want it," she said. "Besides, we may never be to each other again what we once have been."

"That depends upon you," said he, and they went on again as before.

The hired carriers paced along over Chaldon Down with as little hesitation as if it had been day, avoiding the cart-way, and leaving the village of East Chaldon on the left, so as to reach the crest of the hill at a lonely trackless place not far from the ancient earthwork called Round Pound. An hour's brisk walking brought them within sound of the sea, not many hundred yards from Lullstead Cove. Here they paused, and Lizzy and Stockdale came up with them, when they went on together to the verge of the cliff. One of the men now produced an iron bar, which he drove firmly into the soil a yard from the edge, and attached to it a rope that he had uncoiled from his body. They all began to descend, partly stepping, partly sliding down the incline, as the rope slipped through their hands.

"You will not go to the bottom, Lizzy?" said Stockdale, anxiously.

"No; I stay here to watch," she said. "Owlett is down there."

The men remained quite silent when they reached the shore; and the next thing audible to the two at the top was the dip of heavy oars, and the dashing of waves against a boat's bow. In a moment the keel gently touched the shingle, and Stockdale heard the footsteps of the thirty-six carriers running forward over the pebbles towards the point of landing.

There was a sousing in the water as of a brood of ducks plunging in, showing that the men had not been particular about keeping their legs, or even their waists, dry from the brine; but it was impossible to see what they were doing, and in a few minutes the shingle was trampled again. The iron bar sustaining the rope, on which Stockdale's hand rested, began to swerve a little, and the carriers one by one appeared climbing up the sloping cliff, dripping audibly as they came, and sustaining themselves by the guide-rope. Each man on reaching the top was seen to be carrying a pair of tubs, one on his back and one on his chest, the two being slung together by cords passing round the chine hoops, and resting on the carrier's shoulders. Some of the stronger men carried three by putting an extra one on the top behind, but the customary load was a pair, these being quite weighty enough to give their bearer the sensation of having chest and backbone in contact after a walk of four or five miles.

"Where is Owlett?" said Lizzy to one of them.

"He will not come up this way," said the carrier. "He's to bide on shore till we be safe off." Then, without waiting for the rest, the foremost men plunged across the down; and when the last had ascended, Lizzy pulled up the rope, wound it round her arm, wriggled the bar from the sod, and turned to follow the carriers.

"You are very anxious about Owlett's safety," said the minister.

"Was there ever such a man!" said Lizzy. "Why, isn't he my cousin?"

"Yes. Well, it is a bad night's work," said Stockdale, heavily. "But I'll carry the bar and rope for you."

"Thank God, the tubs have got so far all right," said she.

Stockdale shook his head, and, taking the bar, walked by her side towards the down, and the moan of the sea was heard no more.

"Is this what you meant the other day when you spoke of having business with Owlett?" the young man asked.

"This is it," she replied. "I never see him on any other matter."

"A partnership of that kind with a young man is very odd."

"It was begun by my father and his, who were brother-laws."

Her companion could not blind himself to the fact that where tastes and pursuits were so akin as Lizzy's and Owlett's, and where risks were shared, as with them, in every undertaking, there would be a peculiar appropriateness in her answering Owlett's standing question on matrimony in the affirmative. This did not soothe Stockdale, its tendency being rather to stimulate in him an effort to make the pair as inappropriate as possible, and win her away from this nocturnal crew to correctness of conduct and a minister's parlor in some far-removed inland county.

They had been walking near enough to the file of carriers for Stockdale to perceive that, when they got into the road to the village, they split up into two companies of unequal size, each of which made off in a direction of its own. One company, the smaller of the two, went towards the church, and by the time that Lizzy and Stockdale reached their own house these men had scaled the church-yard wall, and were proceeding noiselessly over the grass within.

"I see that Owlett has arranged for one batch to be put in the church again," observed Lizzy. "Do you remember my taking you there the first night you came?"

"Yes, of course," said Stockdale. "No wonder you had permission to broach the tubs—they were his, I suppose?"

"No, they were not—they were mine; I had permission from myself. The day after that they went several miles inland in a wagon-load of manure, and sold very well."

At this moment the group of men who had made off to the left some time before began leaping one by one from the hedge opposite Lizzy's house, and the first man, who had no tubs upon his shoulders, came forward.

"Mrs. Newberry, isn't it?" he said, hastily.

"Yes, Jim," said she. "What's the matter?"

"I find that we can't put any in Badger's Clump tonight, Lizzy," said Owlett. "The place is watched. We must sling the apple-tree in the orchet if there's time. We can't put any more under the church lumber than I have sent on there, and my mixen hev already more in en than is safe."

"Very well," she said. "Be quick about it—that's all. What can I do?"

"Nothing at all, please. Ah, it is the minister!—you two that can't do anything had better get in-doors and not be seed."

While Owlett thus conversed, in a tone so full of contraband anxiety and so free from lover's jealousy, the men who followed him had been descending one by one from the hedge; and it unfortunately happened that when the hindmost took his leap, the cord which sustained his tubs slipped; the result was that both the kegs fell into the road, one of them being stove in by the blow.

"'Od drown it all!" said Owlett, rushing back.

"It is worth a good deal, I suppose?" said Stockdale.

"Oh no—about two guineas and half to us now," said Lizzy, excitedly. "It isn't that—it is the smell! It is so blazing strong before it has been lowered by water that it smells dreadfully when spilled in the road like that! I do hope Latimer won't pass by till it is gone off."

Owlett and one or two others picked up the burst tub and began to scrape and trample over the spot, to disperse the liquor as much as possible; and then they all entered the gate of Owlett's orchard, which adjoined Lizzy's garden on the right. Stockdale did not care to follow them, for several on recognizing him had looked wonderingly at his presence, though they said nothing. Lizzy left his side and went to the bottom of the garden, looking over the hedge into the orchard, where the men could be dimly seen bustling about, and apparently hiding the tubs. All was done noiselessly, and without a light; and when it was over they dispersed in different directions, those who had taken their cargoes to the church having already gone off to their homes.

Lizzy returned to the garden gate, over which Stockdale was still abstractedly leaning. "It is all finished: I am going in-doors now," she said, gently. "I will leave the door ajar for you."

"Oh no, you needn't," said Stockdale; "I am coming too."

But before either of them had moved, the faint clatter of horses' hoofs broke upon the ear, and it seemed to come from the point where the track across the down joined the hard road.

"They are just too late!" cried Lizzy, exultingly.

"Who?" said Stockdale.

"Latimer, the riding-officer, and some assistant of his. We had better go in-doors."

They entered the house, and Lizzy bolted the door. "Please don't get a light, Mr. Stockdale," she said.

"Of course I will not," said he.

"I thought you might be on the side of the King," said Lizzy, with faintest sarcasm.

"I am," said Stockdale. "But, Lizzy Newberry, I love you, and you know it perfectly well; and you ought to know, if you do not, what I have suffered in my conscience on your account these last few days!"

"I guess very well," she said, hurriedly. "Yet I don't see why. Ah, you are better than I!"

The trotting of the horses seemed to have again died away, and the pair of listeners touched each other's fingers in the cold "good-night" of those whom something seriously divided. They were on the landing, but before they had taken three steps apart the tramp of the horsemen suddenly revived, almost close to the house. Lizzy turned to the staircase window, opened the casement about an inch, and put her face close to the aperture. "Yes, one of 'em is Latimer," she whispered. "He always rides a white horse. One would think it was the last color for a man in that line."

Stockdale looked, and saw the white shape of the animal as it passed by; but before the riders had gone another ten yards, Latimer reined in his horse, and said something to his companion which neither Stockdale nor Lizzy could hear. Its drift was, however, soon made evident, for the other man stopped also; and sharply turning the horses' heads they cautiously retraced their steps. When they were again opposite Mrs. Newberry's garden, Latimer dismounted, and the man on the dark horse did the same.

Lizzy and Stockdale, intently listening and observing the proceedings, naturally put their heads as close as possible to the slit formed by the slightly opened casement; and thus it occurred that at last their cheeks came positively into contact. They went on listening, as if they did not know of the singular circumstance which had happened to their faces, and the pressure of each to each rather increased than lessened with the lapse of time.

They could hear the excisemen sniffing the air like hounds as they paced slowly along. When they reached the spot where the tub had burst, both stopped on the instant.

"Ay, ay, 'tis quite strong here," said the second officer. "Shall we knock at the door?"

"Well, no," said Latimer. "Maybe this is only a trick to put us off the scent. They wouldn't kick up this stink anywhere near their hiding-place. I have known such things before."

"Anyhow, the things, or some of 'em, must have been brought this way," said the other.

"Yes," said Latimer, musingly. "Unless 'tis all done to tole us the wrong way. I have a mind that we go home for to-night without saying a word, and come the first thing in the morning with more hands. I know they have storages about here, but we can do nothing by this owl's light. We will look round the parish and see if everybody is in bed, John; and if all is quiet, we will do as I say."

They went on, and the two inside the window could hear them passing leisurely through the whole village, the street of which curved round at the bottom and entered the turnpike road at another junction. This way the excisemen followed, and the amble of their horses died quite away.

"What will you do?" said Stockdale, withdrawing from his position.

She knew that he alluded to the coming search by the officers, to divert her attention from their own tender incident by the casement, which he wished to be passed over as a thing rather dreamed of than done. "Oh, nothing," she replied, with as much coolness as she could command under her disappointment at his manner. "We often have such storms as this. You would not be frightened if you knew what fools they are. Fancy riding o' horseback through the place: of course they will hear and see nobody while they make that noise; but they are always afraid to get off, in case some of our fellows should burst out upon 'em, and tie them up to the gatepost, as they have done before now. Good-night, Mr. Stockdale."

She closed the window and went to her room, where a tear fell from her eyes; and that not because of the alertness of the riding-officers.

CHAPTER VI
THE GREAT SEARCH AT NETHER-MOYNTON

Stockdale was so excited by the events of the evening, and the dilemma that he was placed in between conscience and love, that he did not sleep, or even doze, but remained as broadly awake as at noonday. As soon as the gray light began to touch ever so faintly the whiter objects in his bedroom, he arose, dressed himself, and went down-stairs into the road.

The village was already astir. Several of the carriers had heard the well-known tramp of Latimer's horse while they were undressing in the dark that night, and had already communicated with one another and Owlett on the subject. The only doubt seemed to be about the safety of those tubs which had been left under the church gallery stairs, and after a short discussion at the corner of the mill, it was agreed that these should be removed before it got lighter, and hidden in the middle of a double hedge bordering the adjoining field. However, before anything could be carried into effect, the footsteps of many men were heard coming down the lane from the highway.

"D—— it, here they be," said Owlett, who, having already drawn the hatch and started his mill for the day, stood stolidly at the mill door covered with flour, as if the interest of his whole soul was bound up in the shaking walls around him.

The two or three with whom he had been talking dispersed to their usual work, and when the excise officers and the formidable body of men they had hired reached the village cross, between the mill and Mrs. Newberry's house, the village wore the natural aspect of a place beginning its morning labors.

"Now," said Latimer to his associates, who numbered thirteen men in all, "what I know is that the things are somewhere in this here place. We have got the day before us, and 'tis hard if we can't light upon 'em and get 'em to Budmouth Custom-house before night. First we will try the fuel-houses, and then we'll work our way into the chimmers, and then to the ricks and stables, and so creep round. You have nothing but your noses to guide ye, mind, so use 'em to-day if you never did in your lives before."

Then the search began. Owlett, during the early part, watched from his mill window, Lizzy from the door of her house, with the greatest self-possession. A farmer down below, who also had a share in the run, rode about with one eye on his fields and the other on Latimer and his myrmidons, prepared to put them off the scent if he should be asked a question. Stockdale, who was no smuggler at all, felt more anxiety than the worst of them, and went about his studies with a heavy heart, coming frequently to the door to ask Lizzy some question or other on the consequences to her of the tubs being found.

"The consequences," she said, quietly, "are simply that I shall lose 'em. As I have none in the house or garden, they can't touch me personally."

"But you have some in the orchard?"

"Owlett rents that of me, and he lends it to others. So it will be hard to say who put any tubs there if they should be found."

There was never such a tremendous sniffing known as that which took place in Nether-Moynton parish and its vicinity this day. All was done methodically, and mostly on hands and knees. At different hours of the day they had different plans. From daybreak to breakfast-time the officers used their sense of smell in a direct and straightforward manner only, pausing nowhere but at such places as the tubs might be supposed to be secreted in at that very moment, pending their removal on the following night. Among the places tested and examined were:

Hollow trees.	Cupboards.	Culverts.
Potato-graves.	Clock-cases.	Hedge-rows.
Fuel-houses.	Chimney-flues.	Fagot-ricks.
Bedrooms.	Rain-water butts.	Haystacks.
Apple-lofts.	Pigsties.	Coppers and ovens.

After breakfast they recommenced with renewed vigor, taking a new line; that is to say, directing their attention to clothes that might be supposed to have come in contact with the tubs in their removal from the shore, such garments being usually tainted with the spirits, owing to its oozing between the staves. They now sniffed at

Smock-frocks.	Smiths' and shoemakers' aprons.
Old shirts and waistcoats.	Knee-naps and hedging-gloves.
Coats and hats.	Tarpaulins.
Breeches and leggings.	Market-cloaks.
Women's shawls and gowns.	Scarecrows.

And, as soon as the mid-day meal was over, they pushed their search into places where the spirits might have been thrown away in alarm:

Horse-ponds.	Mixens.	Sinks in yards.
Stable-drains.	Wet ditches.	Road-scrapings.
Cinder-heaps.	Cesspools.	Back-door gutters.

But still these indefatigable excisemen discovered nothing more than the original telltale smell in the road opposite Lizzy's house, which even yet had not passed off.

"I'll tell ye what it is, men," said Latimer, about three o'clock in the afternoon, "we must begin over again. Find them tubs I will."

The men, who had been hired for the day, looked at their hands and knees, muddy with creeping on all fours so frequently, and rubbed their noses, as if they had had almost enough of it; for the quantity of bad air which had passed into each one's nostril had rendered it nearly as insensible as a flue. However, after a moment's hesitation, they prepared to start anew, except three, whose power of smell had quite succumbed under the excessive wear and tear of the day.

By this time not a male villager was to be seen in the parish. Owlett was not at his mill, the farmers were not in their fields, the parson was not in his garden, the smith had left his forge, and the wheelwright's shop was silent.

"Where the divil are the folk gone?" said Latimer,

waking up to the fact of their absence, and looking round. "I'll have 'em up for this! Why don't they come and help us? There's not a man about the place but the Methodist parson, and he's an old woman. I demand assistance in the King's name!"

"We must find the jineral public afore we can demand that," said his lieutenant.

"Well, well, we shall do better without 'em," said Latimer, who changed his moods at a moment's notice. "But there's great cause of suspicion in this silence and this keeping out of sight, and I'll bear it in mind. Now we will go across to Owlett's orchard, and see what we can find there."

Stockdale, who heard this discussion from the garden gate, over which he had been leaning, was rather alarmed, and thought it a mistake of the villagers to keep so completely out of the way. He himself, like the excisemen, had been wondering for the last half-hour what could have become of them. Some laborers were of necessity engaged in distant fields, but the master-workmen should have been at home; though one and all, after just showing themselves at their shops, had apparently gone off for the day. He went in to Lizzy, who sat at a back window sewing, and said, "Lizzy, where are the men?"

Lizzy laughed. "Where they mostly are when they

are run so hard as this." She cast her eyes to heaven. "Up there," she said.

Stockdale looked up. "What—on the top of the church tower?" he asked, seeing the direction of her glance.

"Yes."

"Well, I expect they will soon have to come down," said he, gravely. "I have been listening to the officers, and they are going to search the orchard over again, and then every nook in the church."

Lizzy looked alarmed for the first time. "Will you go and tell our folk?" she said. "They ought to be let know." Seeing his conscience struggling within him like a boiling pot, she added, "No, never mind, I'll go myself."

She went out, descended the garden, and climbed over the church-yard wall at the same time that the preventive-men were ascending the road to the orchard. Stockdale could do no less than follow her. By the time that she reached the tower entrance he was at her side, and they entered together.

Nether-Moynton church- tower was, as in many villages, without a turret, and the only way to the top was by going up to the singers' gallery, and thence ascending by a ladder to a square trap-door in the floor of the bell-loft, above which a permanent ladder was fixed, passing through the bells to a hole in the roof. When Lizzy and

Stockdale reached the gallery and looked up, nothing but the trap-door and the five holes for the bell-ropes appeared. The ladder was gone.

"There's no getting up," said Stockdale.

"Oh yes, there is," said she. "There's an eye looking at us at this moment through a knot-hole in that trap-door."

And as she spoke the trap opened, and the dark line of the ladder was seen descending against the white-washed wall. When it touched the bottom Lizzy dragged it to its place, and said, "If you'll go up, I'll follow."

The young man ascended, and presently found himself among consecrated bells for the first time in his life, nonconformity having been in the Stockdale blood for some generations. He eyed them uneasily, and looked round for Lizzy. Owlett stood here, holding the top of the ladder. "What, be you really one of us?" said the miller.

"It seems so," said Stockdale, sadly.

"He's not," said Lizzy, who overheard. "He's neither for nor against us. He'll do us no harm."

She stepped up beside them, and then they went on to the next stage, which, when they had clambered over the dusty bell-carriages, was of easy ascent, leading towards the hole through which the pale sky appeared, and into the open air. Owlett remained behind for a moment, to pull up the lower ladder.

"Keep down your heads," said a voice, as soon as they set foot on the flat.

Stockdale here beheld all the missing parishioners, lying on their stomachs on the tower roof, except a few who, elevated on their hands and knees, were peeping through the embrasures of the parapet. Stockdale did the same, and saw the village lying like a map below him, over which moved the figures of the excisemen, each foreshortened to a crab-like object, the crown of his hat forming a circular disk in the centre of him. Some of the men had turned their heads when the young preacher's figure arose among them.

"What, Mr. Stockdale?" said Matt Grey, in a tone of surprise.

"I'd as lief that it hadn't been," said Jim Clarke. "If the pa'son should see him a trespassing here in his tower, 'twould be none the better for we, seeing how a do hate chapel members. He'd never buy a tub of us again, and he's as good a customer as we have got this side o' Warm'll."

"Where is the pa'son?" said Lizzy.

"In his house, to be sure, that he may see nothing of what's going on—where all good folks ought to be, and this young man likewise."

"Well, he has brought some news," said Lizzy. "They are going to search the orchet and church; can we do anything if they should find?"

"Yes," said her cousin Owlett. "That's what we've been talking o', and we have settled our line. Well, be dazed!"

The exclamation was caused by his perceiving that some of the searchers, having got into the orchard, and begun stooping and creeping hither and thither, were pausing in the middle, where a tree smaller than the rest was growing. They drew closer, and bent lower than ever upon the ground.

"Oh, my tubs!" said Lizzy, faintly, as she peered through the parapet at them.

"They have got 'em, a b'lieve," said Owlett.

The interest in the movements of the officers was so keen that not a single eye was looking in any other direction; but at that moment a shout from the church beneath them attracted the attention of the smugglers, as it did also of the party in the orchard, who sprang to their feet and went towards the church-yard wall. At the same time those of the Government men who had entered the church unperceived by the smugglers cried aloud, "Here be some of 'em at last."

The smugglers remained in a blank silence, uncertain whether "some of 'em" meant tubs or men; but again peeping cautiously over the edge of the tower they learnt that tubs were the things descried; and soon these fated articles were brought one by one into the middle of the church-yard from their hiding-place under the gallery stairs.

"They are going to put 'em on Hinton's vault till they find the rest," said Lizzy, hopelessly. The excisemen had, in fact, begun to pile up the tubs on a large stone slab which was fixed there; and when all were brought out from the tower, two or three of the men were left standing by them, the rest of the party again proceeding to the orchard.

The interest of the smugglers in the next manoeuvres of their enemies became painfully intense. Only about thirty tubs had been secreted in the lumber of the tower, but seventy were hidden in the orchard, making up all that they had brought ashore as yet, the remainder of the cargo having been tied to a sinker and dropped overboard for another night's operations. The excisemen, having re-entered the orchard, acted as if they were positive that here lay hidden the rest of the tubs, which they were determined to find before nightfall. They spread themselves out round the field, and advancing on all fours as before, went anew round every apple-tree in the enclosure. The young tree in the middle again led them to pause, and at length the whole company gathered there in a way which signified that a second chain of reasoning had led to the same results as the first.

When they had examined the sod hereabouts for

some minutes, one of the men rose, ran to a disused porch of the church where tools were kept, and returned with the sexton's pickaxe and shovel, with which they set to work.

"Are they really buried there?" said the minister, for the grass was so green and uninjured that it was difficult to believe it had been disturbed. The smugglers were too interested to reply, and presently they saw, to their chagrin, the officers stand two on each side of the tree; and, stooping and applying their hands to the soil, they bodily lifted the tree and the turf around it. The apple-tree now showed itself to be growing in a shallow box, with handles for lifting at each of the four sides. Under the site of the tree a square hole was revealed, and an exciseman went and looked down.

"It is all up now," said Owlett, quietly. "And now all of ye get down before they notice we are here; and be ready for our next move. I had better bide here till dark, or they may take me on suspicion, as 'tis on my ground. I'll be with ye as soon as daylight begins to pink in."

"And I?" said Lizzy.

"You please look to the linchpins and screws; then go in-doors and know nothing at all. The chaps will do the rest."

The ladder was replaced, and all but Owlett descended, the men passing off one by one at the back of the church, and vanishing on their respective errands. Lizzy walked boldly along the street, followed closely by the minister.

"You are going in-doors, Mrs. Newberry?" he said.

She knew from the words "Mrs. Newberry" that the division between them had widened yet another degree.

"I am not going home," she said. "I have a little thing to do before I go in. Martha Sarah will get your tea."

"Oh, I don't mean on that account," said Stockdale. "What *can* you have to do further in this unhallowed affair?"

"Only a little," she said.

"What is that? I'll go with you."

"No, I shall go by myself. Will you please go in-doors? I shall be there in less than an hour."

"You are not going to run any danger, Lizzy?" said the young man, his tenderness reasserting itself.

"None whatever—worth mentioning," answered she, and went down towards the Cross.

Stockdale entered the garden gate, and stood behind it looking on. The excisemen were still busy in the orchard, and at last he was tempted to enter, and watch their proceedings. When he came closer he found that the secret cellar, of whose existence he had been totally unaware, was formed by timbers placed across from side to side about a foot under the ground, and grassed over.

The excisemen looked up at Stockdale's fair and downy countenance, and evidently thinking him above suspicion, went on with their work again. As soon as all the tubs were taken out, they began tearing up the turf, pulling out the timbers, and breaking in the sides, till the cellar was wholly dismantled and shapeless, the apple-tree lying with its roots high to the air. But the hole which had in its time held so much contraband merchandise was never completely filled up, either then or afterwards, a depression in the greensward marking the spot to this day.

CHAPTER VII
THE WALK TO WARM'ELL CROSS; AND AFTERWARDS

As the goods had all to be carried to Budmouth that night, the excisemen's next object was to find horses and carts for the journey, and they went about the village for that purpose. Latimer strode hither and thither with a lump of chalk in his hand, marking broad arrows so vigorously on every vehicle and set of harness that he came across that it seemed as if he would chalk broad arrows on the very hedges and roads. The owner of every conveyance so marked was bound to give it up for Government purposes. Stockdale, who had had enough of the scene, turned in-doors, thoughtful and depressed. Lizzy was already there, having come in at the back, though she had not yet taken off her bonnet. She looked tired, and her mood was not much brighter than his own. They had but little to say to each other; and the minister went away and attempted to read; but at this he could not succeed, and he shook the little bell for tea.

Lizzy herself brought in the tray, the girl having run off into the village during the afternoon, too full of excitement at the proceedings to remember her state of life. However, almost before the sad lovers had said anything to each other, Martha came in in a steaming state.

"Oh, there's such a stoor, Mrs. Newberry and Mr. Stockdale! The King's excisemen can't get the carts ready nohow at all! They pulled Thomas Ballam's, and William Rogers's, and Stephen Sprake's carts into the road, and off came the wheels, and down fell the carts; and they found there was no linchpins in the arms; and then they tried Samuel Shane's wagon, and found that the screws were gone from he, and at last they looked at the dairyman's cart, and he's got none neither! They have gone now to the blacksmith's to get some made, but he's nowhere to be found!"

Stockdale looked at Lizzy, who blushed very slightly, and went out of the room, followed by Martha Sarah; but before they had got through the passage there was a rap at the front door, and Stockdale recognized Latimer's voice addressing Mrs. Newberry, who had turned back.

"For God's sake, Mrs. Newberry, have you seen

Hardman the blacksmith up this way? If we could get hold of him, we'd e'en a'most drag him by the hair of his head to his anvil, where he ought to be."

"He's an idle man, Mr. Latimer," said Lizzy, archly. "What do you want him for?"

"Why, there isn't a horse in the place that has got more than three shoes on, and some have only two. The wagon-wheels be without strakes, and there's no linchpins to the carts. What with that, and the bother about every set of harness being out of order, we sha'n't be off before nightfall—upon my soul we sha'n't. 'Tis a rough lot, Mrs. Newberry, that you've got about you here; but they'll play at this game once too often, mark my words they will! There's not a man in the parish that don't deserve to be whipped."

It happened that Hardman was at that moment a little farther up the lane, smoking his pipe behind a holly-bush. When Latimer had done speaking he went on in this direction, and Hardman, hearing the exciseman's steps, found curiosity too strong for prudence. He peeped out from the bush at the very moment that Latimer's glance was on it. There was nothing left for him to do but to come forward with unconcern.

"I've been looking for you for the last hour!" said Latimer, with a glare in his eye.

"Sorry to hear that," said Hardman. "I've been out

for a stroll, to look for more hid tubs, to deliver 'em up to Gover'ment."

"Oh yes, Hardman, we know it," said Latimer, with withering sarcasm. "We know that you'll deliver 'em up to Gover'ment. We know that all the parish is helping us, and have been all day! Now, you please walk along with me down to your shop, and kindly let me hire ye in the King's name."

They went down the lane together, and presently there resounded from the smithy the ring of a hammer not very briskly swung. However, the carts and horses were got into some sort of travelling condition, but it was not until after the clock had struck six, when the muddy roads were glistening under the horizontal light of the fading day. The smuggled tubs were soon packed into the vehicles, and Latimer, with three of his assistants, drove slowly out of the village in the direction of the port of Budmouth, some considerable number of miles distant, the other excisemen being left to watch for the remainder of the cargo, which they knew to have been sunk somewhere between Ringsworth and Lullstead Cove, and to unearth Owlett, the only person clearly implicated by the discovery of the cave.

Women and children stood at the doors as the carts, each chalked with the Government pitchfork, passed in the increasing twilight; and as they stood they looked at the confiscated property with a melancholy expression that told only too plainly the relation which they bore to the trade.

"Well, Lizzy," said Stockdale, when the crackle of the wheels had nearly died away. "this is a fit finish to your adventure. I am truly thankful that you have got off without suspicion, and the loss only of the liquor. Will you sit down and let me talk to you?"

"By-and-by," she said. "But I must go out now."

"Not to that horrid shore again?" he said, blankly.

"No, not there. I am only going to see the end of this day's business."

He did not answer to this, and she moved towards the door slowly, as if waiting for him to say something more.

"You don't offer to come with me," she added at last. "I suppose that's because you hate me after all this?"

"Can you say it, Lizzy, when you know I only want to save you from such practices? Come with you? Of course I will, if it is only to take care of you. But why will you go out again?"

"Because I cannot rest in-doors. Something is happening, and I must know what. Now, come!" And they went into the dusk together.

When they reached the turnpike-road she turned to the right, and he soon perceived that they were following the direction of the excisemen and their loads. He had given her his arm, and every now and then she suddenly pulled it back, to signify that he was to halt a moment and listen. They had walked rather quickly along the first quarter of a mile, and on the second or third time of standing still she said, "I hear them ahead—don't you?"

"Yes," he said; "I hear the wheels. But what of that?"

"I only want to know if they get clear away from the neighborhood."

"Ah," said he, a light breaking upon him. "Something desperate is to be attempted—and now I remember, there was not a man about the village when we left."

"Hark!" she murmured. The noise of the cart-wheels had stopped, and given place to another sort of sound.

"'Tis a scuffle!" said Stockdale. "There'll be murder! Lizzy, let go my arm; I am going on. On my conscience, I must not stay here and do nothing!"

"There'll be no murder, and not even a broken head," she said. "Our men are thirty to four of them: no harm will be done at all."

"Then there *is* an attack!" exclaimed Stockdale; "and you knew it was to be. Why should you side with men who break the laws like this?"

"Why should you side with men who take from country traders what they have honestly bought wi' their own money in France?" said she, firmly.

"They are not honestly bought," said he.

"They are," she contradicted. "I and Owlett and the others paid thirty shillings for every one of the tubs before they were put on board at Cherbourg, and if a king who is nothing to us sends his people to steal our property, we have a right to steal it back again."

Stockdale did not stop to argue the matter, but went quickly in the direction of the noise, Lizzy keeping at his side. "Don't you interfere, will you, dear Richard?" she said, anxiously, as they drew near. "Don't let us go any closer; 'tis at Warm'ell Cross where they are seizing 'em. You can do no good, and you may meet with a hard blow!"

"Let us see first what is going on," he said. But before they had got much farther the noise of the cart-wheels began again, and Stockdale soon found that they were coming towards him. In another minute the three carts came up, and Stockdale and Lizzy stood in the ditch to let them pass.

Instead of being conducted by four men, as had happened when they went out of the village, the horses and carts were now accompanied by a body of from twenty to thirty, all of whom, as Stockdale perceived to his astonishment, had blackened faces. Among them walked six or eight huge female figures, whom, from their wide strides, Stockdale guessed to be men in disguise. As soon as the party discerned Lizzy and her companion four or five fell back, and when the carts had passed came close to the pair.

"There is no walking up this way for the present," said one of the gaunt women, who wore curls a foot long, dangling down the sides of her face, in the fashion of the time. Stockdale recognized this lady's voice as Owlett's.

"Why not?" said Stockdale. "This is the public highway."

"Now look here, youngster," said Owlett—"oh, 'tis the Methodist parson!—what, and Mrs. Newberry! Well, you'd better not go up that way, Lizzy. They've all run off, and folks have got their own again."

The miller then hastened on and joined his comrades. Stockdale and Lizzy also turned back. "I wish all this hadn't been forced upon us," she said, regretfully. "But if those excisemen had got off with the tubs, half the people in the parish would have been in want for the next month or two."

Stockdale was not paying much attention to her words, and he said, "I don't think I can go back like this. Those four poor excisemen may be murdered, for all I know."

"Murdered!" said Lizzy, impatiently. "We don't do murder here."

"Well, I shall go as far as Warm'ell Cross to see,"

said Stockdale, decisively; and without wishing her safe home or anything else, the minister turned back. Lizzy stood looking at him till his form was absorbed in the shades; and then, with sadness, she went in the direction of Nether-Moynton.

The road was lonely, and after nightfall at this time of the year there was often not a passer for hours. Stockdale pursued his way without hearing a sound beyond that of his own footsteps, and in due time he passed beneath the trees of the plantation which surrounded the Warm'ell Cross-road. Before he had reached the point of intersection he heard voices from the thicket.

"Hoi-hoi-hoi! Help! Help!"

The voices were not at all feeble or despairing, but they were unmistakably anxious. Stockdale had no weapon, and before plunging into the pitchy darkness of the plantation he pulled a stake from the hedge to use in case of need. When he got among the trees he shouted, "What's the matter—where are you?"

"Here!" answered the voices; and pushing through the brambles in that direction, he came near the objects of his search.

"Why don't you come forward?" said Stockdale.

"We be tied to the trees."

"Who are you?"

"Poor Will Latimer the exciseman!" said one,

plaintively. "Just come and cut these cords, there's a good man! We were afraid nobody would pass by to-night."

Stockdale soon loosened them, upon which they stretched their limbs and stood at their ease.

"The rascals!" said Latimer, getting now into a rage, though he had seemed quite meek when Stockdale first came up. "'Tis the same set of fellows. I know they were Moynton chaps to a man."

"But we can't swear to 'em," said another. "Not one of 'em spoke."

"What are you going to do?" said Stockdale.

"I'd fain go back to Moynton, and have at 'em again!" said Latimer.

"So would we!" said his comrades.

"Fight till we die!" said Latimer.

"We will, we will!" said his men.

"But," said Latimer, more frigidly, as they came out of the plantation, "we don't *know* that these chaps with black faces were Moynton men. And proof is a hard thing."

"So it is," said the rest.

"And therefore we won't do nothing at all," said Latimer, with complete dispassionateness. "For my part, I'd sooner be them than we. The clitches of my arms are burning like fire from the cords those two strapping women tied round 'em. My opinion is, now I have had time to think o't, that you may serve your gover'ment at too high a price. For these two nights and days I have not had an hour's rest; and, please God, here's for home-along."

The other officers agreed heartily to this course, and thanking Stockdale for his timely assistance, they parted from him at the cross, taking themselves the western road and Stockdale going back to Nether-Moynton.

During that walk the minister was lost in reverie of the most painful kind. As soon as he got into the house, and before entering his own rooms, he advanced to the door of the little back parlor in which Lizzy usually sat with her mother. He found her there alone. Stockdale went forward, and, like a man in a dream, looked down upon the table that stood between him and the young woman, who had her bonnet and cloak still on. As he did not speak, she looked up from her chair at him, with misgiving in her eye.

"Where are they gone?" he then said, listlessly.

"Who?—I don't know. I have seen nothing of them since. I came straight in here."

"If your men can manage to get off with those tubs it will be a great profit to you, I suppose?"

"A share will be mine, a share my cousin Owlett's, a share to each of the two farmers, and a share divided among the men who helped us."

"And you still think," he went on slowly, "that you will not give this business up?"

Lizzy rose, and put her hand upon his shoulder. "Don't ask that," she whispered. "You don't know what you are asking. I must tell you, though I meant not to do it. What I make by that trade is all I have to keep my mother and myself with."

He was astonished. "I did not dream of such a thing," he said. "I would rather have swept the streets, had I been you. What is money compared with a clear conscience?"

"My conscience is clear. I know my mother, but the King I have never seen. His dues are nothing to me. But it is a great deal to me that my mother and I should live."

"Marry me, and promise to give it up. I will keep your mother."

"It is good of you," she said, trembling a little. "Let me think of it by myself. I would rather not answer now."

She reserved her answer till the next day, and came into his room with a solemn face. "I cannot do what you wished!" she said, passionately. "It is too much to ask. My whole life ha' been passed in this way." Her words and manner showed that before entering she had been struggling with herself in private, and that the contention had been strong.

Stockdale turned pale, but he spoke quietly. "Then, Lizzy, we must part. I cannot go against my principles in this matter, and I cannot make my profession a mockery. You know how I love you, and what I would do for you; but this one thing I cannot do."

"But why should you belong to that profession?" she burst out. "I have got this large house; why can't you marry me, and live here with us, and not be a Methodist preacher any more? I assure you, Richard, it is no harm, and I wish you could only see it as I do! We only carry it on in winter; in summer it is never done at all. It stirs up one's dull life at this time o' the year, and gives excitement, which I have got so used to now that I should hardly know how to do 'ithout it. At nights, when the wind blows, instead of being dull and stupid, and not noticing whether it do blow or not, your mind is afield, even if you are not afield yourself; and you are wondering how the chaps are getting on; and you walk up and down the room, and look out o' window, and then you go out yourself, and know your way about as well by night as by day, and have hair-breadth escapes from old Latimer and his fellows, who are too stupid ever to really frighten us, and only make us a bit nimble."

"He frightened you a little last night, anyhow; and I would advise you to drop it before it is worse."

She shook her head. "No, I must go on as I have begun. I was born to it. It is in my blood, and I can't be cured. Oh, Richard, you cannot think what a hard thing you have asked, and how sharp you try me when you put me between this and my love for 'ee!"

Stockdale was leaning with his elbow on the mantelpiece, his hands over his eyes. "We ought never to have met, Lizzy," he said. "It was an ill day for us. I little thought there was anything so hopeless and impossible in our engagement as this. Well, it is too late now to regret consequences in this way. I have had the happiness of seeing you and knowing you at least."

"You dissent from Church, and I dissent from State," she said, "and I don't see why we are not well matched."

He smiled sadly, while Lizzy remained looking down, her eyes beginning to overflow.

That was an unhappy evening for both of them, and the days that followed were unhappy days. Both she and he went mechanically about their employments, and his depression was marked in the village by more than one of his denomination with whom he came in contact. But Lizzy, who passed her days in-doors, was unsuspected of being the cause: for it was generally understood that a quiet engagement to marry existed between her and her cousin Owlett, and had existed for some time.

Thus uncertainly the week passed on, till one morning Stockdale said to her, "I have had a letter, Lizzy. I must call you that till I am gone."

"Gone?" said she, blankly.

"Yes," he said. "I am going from this place. I felt it would be better for us both that I should not stay after what has happened. In fact, I couldn't stay here, and look on you from day to day, without becoming weak and faltering in my course. I have just heard of an arrangement by which the other minister can arrive here in about a week, and let me go elsewhere."

That he had all this time continued so firmly fixed in his resolution came upon her as a grievous surprise. "You never loved me!" she said, bitterly.

"I might say the same," he returned; "but I will not. Grant me one favor. Come and hear my last sermon on the day before I go."

Lizzy, who was a church-goer on Sunday mornings, frequently attended Stockdale's chapel in the evening with the rest of the double-minded, and she promised.

It became known that Stockdale was going to leave, and a good many people outside his own sect were sorry to hear it. The intervening days flew rapidly away, and on the evening of the Sunday which preceded the morning of his departure Lizzy sat in the chapel to hear him for the last time. The little building was full to overflowing, and he took up the subject which all had expected, that of the contraband trade so extensively practised among them. His hearers, in laying his words to their own hearts, did not perceive that they were most particularly directed against Lizzy, till the sermon waxed warm and Stockdale nearly broke down with emotion. In truth, his own earnestness, and her sad eyes looking up at him, were too much for the young man's equanimity. He hardly knew how he ended. He saw Lizzy, as through a mist, turn and go away with the rest of the congregation, and shortly afterwards followed her home.

She invited him to supper, and they sat down alone, her mother having, as was usual with her on Sunday nights, gone to bed early.

"We will part friends, won't we?" said Lizzy, with forced gayety, and never alluding to the sermon—a reticence which rather disappointed him.

"We will," he said, with a forced smile on his part; and they sat down.

It was the first meal that they had ever shared together in their lives, and probably the last that they would so share. When it was over, and the indifferent conversation could no longer be continued, he arose and took her hand. "Lizzy," he said, "do you say we must part—do you?"

"You do," she said, solemnly. "I can say no more."

"Nor I," said he. "If that is your answer, good-by!"

Stockdale bent over her and kissed her, and she involuntarily returned his kiss. "I shall go early," he said, hurriedly. "I shall not see you again."

And he did leave early. He fancied, when stepping forth into the gray morning light, to mount the van which was to carry him away, that he saw a face between the parted curtains of Lizzy's window; but the light was faint, and the panes glistened with wet; so he could not be sure. Stockdale mounted the vehicle, and was gone; and on the following Sunday the new minister preached in the chapel of the Moynton Wesleyans.

One day, two years after the parting, Stockdale, now settled in a midland town, came into Nether-Moynton by carrier in the original way. Jogging along in the van that afternoon, he had put questions to the driver, and the answers that he received interested the minister deeply. The result of them was that he went without the least hesitation to the door of his former lodging. It was about six o'clock in the evening, and the same time of year as when he had left; now, too, the ground was damp and glistening, the west was bright, and Lizzy's snow-drops were raising their heads in the border under the wall.

Lizzy must have caught sight of him from the window, for by the time that he reached the door she was there holding it open; and then, as if she had not sufficiently considered her act of coming out, she drew herself back, saying, with some constraint, "Mr. Stockdale!"

"You knew it was," said Stockdale, taking her hand. "I wrote to say I should call."

"Yes, but you did not say when," she answered.

"I did not. I was not quite sure when my business would lead me to these parts."

"You only came because business brought you near?"

"Well, that is the fact; but I have often thought I should like to come on purpose to see you. But what's all this that has happened? I told you how it would be, Lizzy, and you would not listen to me."

"I would not," she said, sadly. "But I had been brought up to that life, and it was second nature to me. However, it is all over now. The officers have blood-money for taking a man dead or alive, and the trade is going to nothing. We were hunted down like rats."

"Owlett is quite gone, I hear."

"Yes, he is in America. We had a dreadful struggle that last time, when they tried to take him. It is a perfect miracle that he lived through it; and it is a wonder that I was not killed. I was shot in the hand. It was not by aim; the shot was really meant for my cousin; but I was behind, looking on as usual, and the bullet came to me. It bled terribly, but I got home without fainting, and it healed after a time. You know how he suffered?"

"No," said Stockdale. "I only heard that he just escaped with his life."

"He was shot in the back, but a rib turned the ball. He was badly hurt. We would not let him be took. The men carried him all night across the meads to Bere, and hid him in a barn, dressing his wound as well as they could, till he was so far recovered as to be able to get about. He had gied up his mill for some time, and at last he got to Bristol, and took a passage to America, and he's settled in Wisconsin."

"What do you think of smuggling now?" said the minister, gravely.

"I own that we were wrong," said she. "But I have suffered for it. I am very poor now, and my mother has been dead these twelve months. But won't you come in, Mr. Stockdale?"

Stockdale went in; and it is to be presumed that they came to an understanding, for a fortnight later there was a sale of Lizzy's furniture, and after that a wedding at a chapel in a neighboring town.

He took her away from her old haunts to the home that he had made for himself in his native county, where she studied her duties as a minister's wife with praiseworthy assiduity. It is said that in after-years she wrote an excellent tract called "Render unto Caesar; or, The Repentant Villagers," in which her own experience was anonymously used as the introductory story. Stockdale got it printed, after making some corrections, and putting in a few powerful sentences of his own; and many hundreds of copies were distributed by the couple in the course of their married life.

April 1879.